PAUL BUNYAN

Adapted by **Stephen Krensky**
Illustrations by **Craig Orback**

M Millbrook Press/Minneapolis

Millbrook Press, Inc.
A division of Lerner Publishing Group
241 First Avenue North
Minneapolis, MN 55401

Website address: www.lernerbooks.com

Library of Congress Cataloging-in-Publication Data

Krensky, Stephen.
    Paul Bunyan / adapted by Stephen Krensky ; illustrated by Craig Orback.
        p.   cm. — (On my own folklore)
    Summary: Relates some of the exploits of Paul Bunyan, a lumberjack said to be
    taller than the trees whose pet was a blue ox named Babe.
    ISBN-13: 978–1–57505–888–7 (lib. bdg. : alk. paper)
    ISBN-10: 1–57505–888–X (lib. bdg. : alk. paper)
    1. Bunyan, Paul (Legendary character)—Legends. [1. Bunyan, Paul (Legendary
character)—Legends. 2. Folklore—United States. 3. Tall tales.] I. Orback, Craig, ill.
II. Title.
PZ8.1.K8663Pau 2007
398.20973'02—dc22   2005033157

Manufactured in the United States of America
1 2 3 4 5 6 – JR – 12 11 10 09 08 07

for Shannon Barefield
—S.K.

for my friend Wing,
who set me on this path
—C.S.O.

Paul Bunyan: A Folklore Hero

Maybe you have heard of Paul Bunyan. Perhaps some-
one has mentioned his name, or you have heard a story.
Paul Bunyan is one of America's tall-tale heroes. Stories
about him come to us from the lumber camps of the
northern United States. In those camps, workers known
as lumberjacks cleared the forests to make room for
pioneer houses and farms. Those workers from long ago
may have told the first stories about Paul.

We call stories like Paul's tall tales because every-
thing in them is extra big, extra fast, and extra wild.
And the truth in these stories might be just a bit
stretched. The heroes and heroines in tall tales are as
tall as buildings, as strong as oxen, or as fast as light-
ning. They meet with wild adventures at every turn.
But that's okay, because they can solve just about every
problem that comes their way.

Tale tales may be funny and outsized. But they de-
scribe the life that many workers and pioneers shared.
The people in these stories have jobs that real people
had. And the stories are always set in familiar places.

The first tellers of these tales may have known these
people and places. Or they may have wished they could
be just like the hero in the story. The stories were told
again and again and passed from person to person. We
call such spoken and shared stories folklore.

Folklore is the stories and customs of a place or a people. Folklore can be folktales like the tall tale. These stories are usually not written down until much later, after they have been told and retold for many years. Folklore can also be sayings, jokes, and songs.

Folklore can teach us something. A rhyme or a song may help us remember an event from long ago. Or it may be just for fun, such as a good ghost story or a jump-rope song. Folklore can also tell us about the people who share the stories.

Paul Bunyan's story tells us about life in the lumber camps. It shows how hard the lumberjacks worked and how they had fun. As their hero, Paul has the adventurous spirit of a pioneer. Tales of his deeds quickly spread from the lumber camps through the great woods and beyond. And we tell his story still.

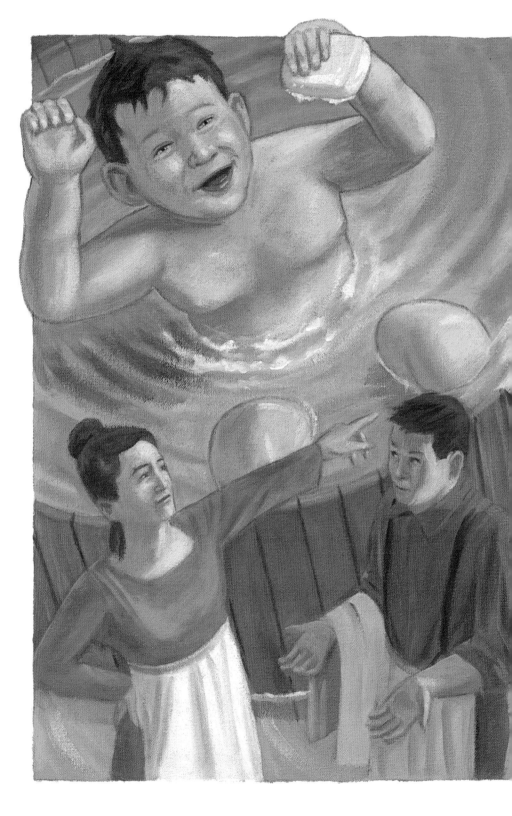

Growing Up

Paul Bunyan was always big.
When he was born,
his first cries broke every window
for miles around.
And that was only the beginning.
His crib was a rowboat with rockers,
and his baths flooded the house
until his parents gave up
and started washing him outside.

But Paul wasn't done growing,
not by a long shot.
It took the wool
from a whole flock of sheep
just to knit him one sweater.
By the time he started school,
he wore potato sacks for socks
and used wagon wheels
to button his shirts.

Of course, so much growing
made Paul hungry.
He ate forty bowls of porridge
for breakfast.
And by the time
he was done cleaning up,
he was hungry all over again.

Paul spent a lot of time in the woods.
He made friends with many animals—
especially the beavers.
Only the bears got mad at him,
because whenever they wrestled him,
Paul always won.

Still, some things were hard for Paul.
He tried to fit in, but it wasn't easy.
The other children could play with him
better than he could play with them.

When Paul was fifteen,
the winter was so cold
even the snow turned blue.
One morning, Paul found a young ox
half-buried in a snowdrift.
If that wasn't odd enough,
the ox was as blue as the snow itself.
"My poor little babe," he said.
And that's how Babe got his name.
Paul never found out
where Babe came from.
But it didn't matter.
Paul was just happy
to have a new friend.

Babe was really strong.
In one of their first jobs,
Paul hitched him up to a crooked road
that needed fixing.
"Pull!" he said.
And Babe pulled.
The road was pretty stubborn,
but so were Paul and Babe.
By the time the sun set,
they had that road
straightened out just fine.
"Good work!" Paul said to Babe,
and Babe snorted back.
They made a good team.

Starting Out

Paul was always comfortable
holding an ax.
With his very first swing,
he cut down a half-grown pine tree.
He used it to brush his hair
until the needles fell out.
When he got older,
Paul decided to be a lumberjack.
At first, he had only Babe to help him.
Paul cut down the trees,
and Babe pulled them into stacks
beside the river.

But there was more work to be done,
more than even Paul
and Babe could do.
So Paul hired himself a crew.
His most famous workers
were his seven axmen—all named Elmer.

Each Elmer weighed over 300 pounds
and was over six feet tall sitting down.
The Elmers didn't chop wood
with regular axes.
They worked faster
twirling the blades around them.

Johnny Inkslinger kept track of things
in the logging camp office.
There was so much figuring to be done,
he invented a pen connected directly
to an ink barrel.
That way, he didn't lose time
filling it up every minute or so.
One week, Johnny was short of ink,
and he saved twelve barrels
by not crossing his t's
or dotting his i's.

Lucy, the Purple Cow,
gave Paul milk, cheese, and butter.
She was happy
as long as the grass was green.
But green grass was hard to come by
in cold weather.
So during the winter months,
Paul had Lucy wear green glasses
to make the snow look like grass.

Sourdough Sam, the cook,
fed Paul's logging crews.
Sam's soup kettle was so big,
he had to row a boat out to the center.
At dinner, his cookhouse boys
wore roller skates
to get from one end of the dining tables
to the other.

The axmen ate hundreds of flapjacks.
Sourdough Sam was always running out
of space to make them.
So, Ole the Blacksmith made a new griddle.
A dozen men skated on bacon slabs to grease it.
At first, the flapjacks in the middle
were too hard to reach.
Then Sam added popcorn to the batter
so the flapjacks flipped themselves.

It was a good thing
Paul and his men kept up their strength.
They faced some strange things
in the wilderness.
One time, they floated some logs
down the Round River.
They didn't give the name much thought.
But pretty soon, they noticed
that they were going in circles.
Paul was starting to get dizzy,
so he dug out the center of the river
and turned Round River into Round Lake.

Another time, the loggers were
buzzed by mosquitoes as big as eagles.
Their stingers were very nasty.
Paul finally swatted them all
out into the ocean.
They got lost there and never
found their way back.

The Year of the Two Winters

It was always cold in the winter.

The lumberjacks were used to that.

But one year was much colder than the rest.

Maybe Paul should have seen it coming.

The leaves that fall didn't turn red or yellow.

They turned dark blue from the cold.

Once the snow started falling,
it just wouldn't quit.
At first, the lumberjacks cut new paths
through the fresh snow every day.
But after a while,
they let the snow pile up
and dug tunnels under it instead.
After a month, the snow got so deep
Paul had to dig down
just to find the treetops.

Looking back, they called it
the Year of the Two Winters.
By January, the icicles had reached the ground
and started to take root.
Shadows froze against walls
and couldn't get loose.
Lucy's milk turned to ice cream
before it hit the pail.
And lighting fires was no good
because the flames froze solid.
They were pretty to look at
but weren't worth a lick for warmth.

Of course, things weren't all bad.
It was so cold
even the bedbugs
huddled together
to keep warm.
Scooping them up was quick and easy,
so the lumberjacks
had clean sheets for once.

Nobody got any work done
because keeping warm
was pretty much a full-time job.
The lumberjacks let their beards
grow and grow and grow.
They wrapped them around like scarves.
Even the snowmen
needed more clothes than usual.

When spring came,
Paul cut everyone's beard.
The whiskers were stacked up
and later stuffed into mattresses.
The cracking of the ice
went on for weeks.
The only people who got any sleep
wore three pairs of earmuffs to bed.
But nobody complained.
They were just glad
things were back to normal.

Moving On

Paul and Babe were happy
the long winter was over.
After being cooped up for so long,
they were eager to stretch their legs.
Paul hitched a plow to Babe,
and they dug a groove from Round Lake
down to the Gulf of Mexico.
As the water rushed south,
it made a nice wide river.
Paul called it the Mississippi.
He piled the dirt neatly on one side.
There were a lot of stones
and boulders mixed in.
When he was done,
he called the whole pile
the Rocky Mountains.

On their way back north,

Paul and Babe walked through the desert.

It was terribly hot,

and Paul took to dragging

his great ax behind him.

The heavy ax cut deeply into the soft sand.

At sunset, Paul turned to look behind him.

"What a grand canyon!" Paul said,

and the name stuck after that.

Back home, Paul found his loggers
scratching their heads.
They had piled too many logs
into the river.
Now the logs were stuck
in a mile-long jam.
Paul thought over the problem a minute.
Then he told everyone to stand back.
He put Babe in front of the jam
and tickled his back with a pine tree.
Babe thought a fly was bothering him
and flicked his tail back and forth.
Each time his tail hit the water,
it sent a wave
crashing against the logs.
They were jarred loose ten at a time,
but it still took three days
before the last of them broke free.

Paul and his lumberjacks kept so busy
that one day there were no more trees
worth cutting down.
Some of the loggers liked the look
of the cleared land
and decided to settle down.
But not Paul.
He needed more elbow room.
So he and Babe
said good-bye to the loggers
and headed out west.

No one knows where they ended up,
and Paul was careful
not to leave any footprints behind.
But every time you see a big mountain
or a deep canyon
or a rushing river,
you know these things
don't happen by themselves.
So it's a pretty good bet
that Paul Bunyan was there before you.

Further Reading and Websites

American Folklore
  http://www.americanfolklore.net/
  This folklore website features tall tales, ghost stories, regional legends,
  and famous characters.
Kurelek, William. *Lumberjack.* 1974. Reprint, Topeka, KS: Sagebrush
  Education Resources, 1999.
  Kurelek records the traditional life of a lumberjack, in original art and
  text.
Monte, Mike. *Cut and Run: Loggin' Off the Big Woods.* Atglen, PA:
  Schiffer Publishing, 2002.
  More than 150 historical photos highlight this title about the lives of
  loggers in the Upper Great Lakes.
Tales of American Folklore. Logan, IA: Perfection Learning, 2000.
  Tall tales and colorful characters are collected in this book.